POKÉMON™

ALOLA DELUXE ACTIVITY BOOK

This book belongs to:

....

....

Age: ....

My Pokémon buddy:

....

All rights reserved. Published by Scholastic Inc., *Publishers since 1920*. SCHOLASTIC and associated logos
are trademarks and/or registered trademarks of Scholastic Inc.

The publisher does not have any control over and does not assume any responsibility for author
or third-party websites or their content.

No part of this publication may be reproduced, stored in a retrieval system, or transmitted in any form
or by any means, electronic, mechanical, photocopying, recording, or otherwise, without written
permission of the publisher. For information regarding permission, write to Scholastic Inc., Attention:
Permissions Department, 557 Broadway, New York, NY 10012.

This book is a work of fiction. Names, characters, places, and incidents are either the product of the
author's imagination or are used fictitiously, and any resemblance to actual persons, living or dead,
business establishments, events, or locales is entirely coincidental.

ISBN 978-1-338-30472-5

10 9 8 7 6 5 4 3 2 1   19 20 21 22 23

Printed in Malaysia   106
First printing 2019

CONTENTS

WELCOME TO ALOLA!

Greetings from the tropical Alola region, where Ash and Pikachu are exploring the sunny islands in search of new and exciting creatures called Pokémon!

Meet new friends including Professor Kukui, Samson Oak, and expert Trainers: Kiawe, Lana, Mallow, and Sophocles. With rare Mythical and super-powerful Legendary Pokémon, this could be the most exciting chapter yet on Ash's quest to become a Pokémon Master.

Read stories of Ash and Pikachu's adventures, try the puzzles, and learn the key stats and facts to decide which Pokémon will help you win your next battle.

READY?
THEN LET'S GO!

ALOLA, ASH!

Meet Ash Ketchum, a ten-year-old boy from Pallet Town in the Kanto region.

hat

backpack

Poké Ball

Ash has traveled far and wide on his quest to become a Pokémon Master, and his travels have now brought him to the Alola region. Lots of new and exciting Pokémon are waiting to greet Ash on the tropical Alolan islands, and our hero wants to meet them all!

Z-Ring

PIKACHU

Ash's buddy Pikachu is his constant companion on his Alolan adventure. Ash and Pikachu have been best friends since Ash's first days as a Trainer, and the pair have been traveling together ever since.

ROWLET

Grass- and Flying-type Pokémon Rowlet is a loyal friend to Ash. During the day, it sometimes likes to sleep in Ash's backpack, and save its energy for nighttime flights.

ROCKRUFF

Ash first meets Rockruff at Professor Kukui's place, where the playful Rock-type Pokémon takes an instant shine to Ash and Pikachu! Rockruff has a strong sense of smell, which it uses to track down anything or anyone that's missing.

NEW FRIENDS

As well as meeting some amazing Alolan Pokémon, Ash and Pikachu encounter plenty of colorful people on their travels around the region!

PRINCIPAL SAMSON OAK

Samson Oak is the cousin of the famous Professor Oak of Kanto and is the principal of the Pokémon School on Melemele Island. Principal Oak studies regional variants of Pokémon, such as the Alolan Exeggutor. He's an easygoing guy whose favorite hobby is making puns on Pokémon names.

POKÉMON: Komala

PROFESSOR KUKUI

Professor Kukui is the Alola region's coolest professor. What he doesn't know about Pokémon isn't worth knowing! Kukui's special subject is Pokémon moves. He's not the type of teacher to be stuck in a lab and much prefers to carry out his studies in the field. Rockruff is his trusty companion.

POKÉMON: Rockruff

LILLIE

Lillie is Professor Kukui's assistant. She's not a fan of fighting and would rather read a book than have a Pokémon battle. When Ash first meets her, she even seems scared of Pokémon! Lillie avoids touching Pokémon if she can help it—until she hatches her own Alolan Vulpix.

POKÉMON: Alolan Vulpix

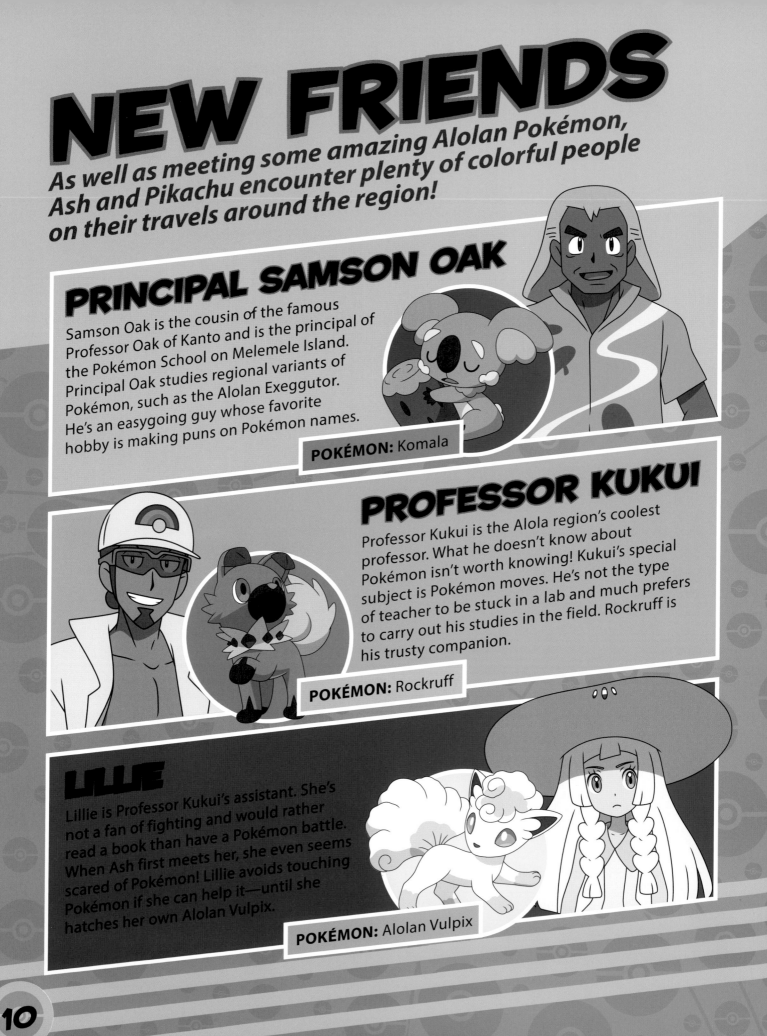

MALLOW

Mallow is a friendly girl who knows pretty much everything about Grass-type Pokémon. She acts as a big sister to Lana and Lillie and welcomes Ash and Pikachu to the island. Her family owns the local eatery where Mallow sometimes helps out—she can make a mean meal for people and Pokémon!

POKÉMON: Bounsweet

LANA

Water-type champion Lana is a quiet girl who looks up to Mallow as a big sister. She lives in a household of fishermen, with her grandmother, parents, and younger twin sisters. She's much less shy at home, but can sometimes show her stubborn streak.

POKÉMON: Popplio

SOPHOCLES

Sophocles, the Electric-type specialist, is another of Ash's school companions. He just loves anything electrical, and is especially curious about computers. He often uses Electric-type Pokémon to power his inventions. Sophocles would love to take apart Rotom Pokédex and improve it if he could!

POKÉMON: Togedemaru

KIAWE

Confident Kiawe is Alola's Fire-type champion and the most experienced Trainer of Ash's new friends. Kiawe studies at the Pokémon School and wears a Z-Ring that allows him to perform some awesome Z-Moves in Pokémon battles! His Air-Ride Pokémon is a Charizard, which he uses to make deliveries around Alola.

POKÉMON: Turtonator

PIKACHU PUZZLER

Pikachu is feeling all mixed up! Rearrange the letters to complete the picture.

A B C D E F G H I J

1 2 3 4 5 6

7 8 9 10

The answers are on page 78.

ALOLA MAZE

Guide Ash and Pikachu through this tricky Poké Ball maze to reach their Trainer friends on the other side! How quickly can you find the finish?

START

FINISH

The answer is on page 78.

13

PUZZLING POKÉ BALLS

What color is a Great Ball and when might Ash or Kiawe use a Master Ball? Read about the different Poké Balls, then color them in using the code below.

Poké Ball

This is the standard Poké Ball that Trainers use to catch Pokémon.

Great Ball

The Great Ball has a greater rate of success in catching Pokémon than the Poké Ball.

Ultra Ball

Throwing an Ultra Ball is even more likely to help you catch a Pokémon than the Poké Ball or Great Ball!

Dusk Ball

Use the Dusk Ball to snare Pokémon at night and in caves.

Repeat Ball

This Poké Ball works well on Pokémon that have been caught before.

Luxury Ball

A Pokémon caught with the Luxury Ball becomes more attached to its Trainer.

Master Ball

The super rare Master Ball guarantees a catch! Save it for a sighting of a Mythical or Legendary Pokémon.

Dive Ball

The Dive Ball comes in handy when trying to catch Pokémon that live in the water.

Quick Ball

When you encounter a Pokémon in the wild, throw this ball first and you have a better chance of catching it.

Net Ball

Choose a Net Ball to catch any Water- and Bug-type Pokémon.

Heal Ball

A good choice to heal any injured Pokémon.

ALOLA TO NEW ADVENTURE!

Ash and Pikachu were on vacation on Melemele, an island in the Alola region, and they were having a blast! With so much to see and do, Ash didn't want the vacation to end.

After a busy day, the pair went to find Ash's mom, Delia, back at the hotel.

"We went underwater with the Sharpedo and saw lots of Pokémon I've never seen before!" Ash told his mom excitedly.

"That sounds like fun!" Delia smiled. "Now, shall we change and get going?"

Ash looked puzzled.

"To Professor Oak's cousin's place?" Delia reminded her son.

Pikachu and Mr. Mime began to cheer.

Before their vacation, Professor Oak had given Delia and Ash a Pokémon Egg to take to the professor's cousin in the Alola region. Ash had begged Professor Oak to tell him what kind of Pokémon it was, but Professor Oak had said that Ash must wait until it hatched to find out.

Everything on Melemele was exciting—even the Pokémon taxis! The taxi arrived at the marketplace, and everyone got out.

As Delia went to look at a stall selling delicious fruit, something caught Ash's eye across the street: a Grubbin!

"It's a Pokémon! I wonder what its name is," Ash said, dashing over to a flower bed. "Let's catch it, Pikachu!"

But Grubbin was too fast. After nipping Ash on the nose, it tunneled away quickly. Ash and Pikachu followed it into a forest, where Ash made a grab for the Grubbin, but the slippery Pokémon escaped.

Ash and Pikachu walked deeper into the forest. Soon, they saw another Pokémon—an enormous Bewear!

"Look, it's waving!" Ash laughed, waving back. "You sure are cute."

Ash had never seen a Bewear before—he didn't know that it wasn't as friendly as it looked.

As he and Pikachu approached it, the Pokémon went wild, spinning into trees and smashing each trunk with its giant paws.

Ash and Pikachu turned and fled back through the forest. They didn't stop running until they were safe.

"What *was* that thing?" panted Ash.

Just then, a Charizard flew over their heads with a male rider on board. "Awesome! Pikachu, let's follow it!"

"*Pika*!" cried Pikachu excitedly.

They burst through some bushes, and found themselves outside a beautiful building. Standing there was a girl dressed in white, with three unfamiliar Pokémon beside her.

Ash and Pikachu ran over to them, but they didn't see the herd of terrifying Tauros racing toward them! They leaped out of the way just in time.

"Are you okay?" the girl gasped.

One of the Tauros riders rushed over. "I'm sorry! You came out of the forest so quickly . . . I couldn't stop," she apologized.

"I'm Ash Ketchum," Ash introduced himself. "I'm from Pallet Town, in the Kanto region. This is my good buddy, Pikachu. Nice to meet you all!"

"*Pika! Pika!*" Pikachu squeaked.

"What is this place?" asked Ash.

"It's the Pokémon School," a girl called Mallow replied. "Pokémon and students study together here. I'll show you around."

Ash and Pikachu followed Mallow inside.

"Principal, sir? I brought a new student," Mallow called, knocking on a classroom door.

Ash was pretty surprised when his mother and Mr. Mime opened the door to greet him! Ash's mom had come to deliver the Egg. A man appeared behind them, too. He looked very familiar to Ash.

"Alola, Ash! Welcome to the Pokémon School," the man smiled.

"Professor Oak? What are you doing here?" Ash gasped.

The man laughed. "People tell me we look alike. The name's *Samson* Oak," he told Ash.

"The Pokémon School principal," Mallow explained.

Ash and his mom sat down with Mallow to catch up on the day's events, while Principal Oak made a video call.

"Hey, Samuel! I got your Egg, safe and sound!" he told his cousin.

"Excellent, Samson! And thank you, Delia." Professor Oak smiled.

A little later, Mallow continued the tour. All the classrooms had views of the ocean. Ash was impressed!

Just then, a young man, wearing a lab coat, shorts, and a baseball cap walked in.

"Professor Kukui," Mallow said, "meet Ash and Pikachu."

"Hi, Ash, Pikachu. The Pokémon School is a wonderful place. Enjoy your visit," he said.

"Thank you," Ash replied.

"*Pika!*" added Pikachu politely.

Suddenly, there were raised voices outside. A group of kids in black were picking on another student—the boy Ash had seen riding a Charizard earlier!

"Who are those guys?" asked Ash.

"They're part of Team Skull," groaned Mallow. "They're always bullying us into Pokémon Battles."

Mallow, Ash, Pikachu, and Professor Kukui headed outside.

"When we beat you, that Charizard of yours will be ours!" one bully jeered to the boy.

Team Skull threw their Poké Balls into the air, calling their Pokémon into action. The battle was on!

"Three against one? You're cowards!" Ash cried, rushing to help.

"What are *you* going to do about it?" a girl sneered.

"I'll fight, too!" Ash smiled. He turned to the other boy, who introduced himself as Kiawe.

Mallow tried to warn Ash, but he was determined to join the battle.

"Pikachu! I choose you!" Ash began.

Then Kiawe threw his Poké Ball, shouting, "Now, Turtonator, come on OUT!"

Ash gasped as a huge, spiked creature appeared.

"Turtonator, a Fire- and Dragon-type. A strong and trusted friend," Kiawe told him.

Team Skull struck back with Salandit, Yungoos, and Zubat, but their plan backfired. As their Pokémon leaped onto Turtonator's back, there was a huge explosion. Team Skull stood back in shock.

"Quick, Salandit, use Flame Burst!" Team Skull tried to fight back.

"Pikachu, dodge and use Thunderbolt!" Ash instructed.

Pikachu moved quickly, and Salandit was dazed.

"I'll finish this. Turtonator, let's go!" Kiawe said. "The zenith of my mind . . . and body . . . and spirit! Become a raging fire and burn! Inferno Overdrive!"

Kiawe had used his special move—Team Skull's Pokémon were beaten!

"We won't forget this!" one of the bullies called. "You should have told us you were going to use a Z-Move!"

Professor Kukui explained that Z-Moves were special moves passed down in Alola. "Each island has its own guardian Pokémon. Only those who participate in a ceremony called the island challenge are able to use Z-Moves," he added.

"Wow!" exclaimed Ash. "Wait, who's that Pokémon?"

But none of the others could see anything.

"It was just there! A yellow Pokémon, with an orange crest!" Ash described.

"That sounds like Tapu Koko, Guardian of Melemele Island," Kukui said.

Later, Ash and his mom were catching up over dinner.

"Everything okay, Ash?" Delia asked. "You seem a little distracted."

Delia was right—Ash's head was spinning with all the cool stuff he'd seen and done that day. He really wanted to catch another glimpse of Tapu Koko.

Suddenly, *"CAW! CAW!"* came a noise from the sky.

"There it is!" cried Ash. He jumped up from his chair and followed the sound, with Pikachu right behind.

"Why do you keep coming to me?" Ash asked Tapu Koko. "Is there something you want to tell me?"

Tapu Koko raised its wing and sent a silver bracelet floating through the air toward Ash.

"Pika?" cried Pikachu.

"That looks like what Kiawe was wearing!" said Ash.

As he reached for the bracelet, blasts of golden light filled the air. Ash snapped the bracelet onto his wrist, and the light beams vanished . . . along with Tapu Koko! What Ash didn't know was that he was now wearing a Z-Ring.

Ash and Pikachu weren't ready for their vacation to end. Ash was sure there were more exciting adventures to come! Now all he had to do was to persuade his mom to let him enroll as a student at the Pokémon School . . . ***Their Alola journey continues on page 50***.

ALOLAN A-Z

Ash and Pikachu meet plenty of new Pokémon and exciting Ultra Beasts on their travels around the Alola region, from the battling Bewear to the sharp-toothed Yungoos. Read on to meet them!

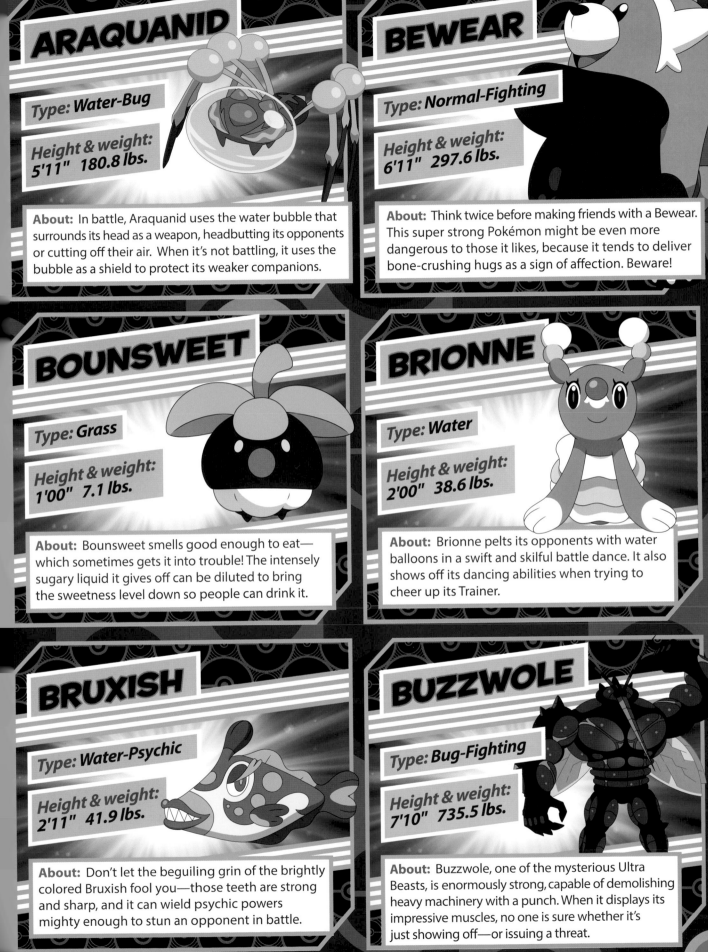

ARAQUANID

Type: *Water-Bug*

Height & weight:
5'11"   180.8 lbs.

About: In battle, Araquanid uses the water bubble that surrounds its head as a weapon, headbutting its opponents or cutting off their air. When it's not battling, it uses the bubble as a shield to protect its weaker companions.

BEWEAR

Type: *Normal-Fighting*

Height & weight:
6'11"   297.6 lbs.

About: Think twice before making friends with a Bewear. This super strong Pokémon might be even more dangerous to those it likes, because it tends to deliver bone-crushing hugs as a sign of affection. Beware!

BOUNSWEET

Type: *Grass*

Height & weight:
1'00"   7.1 lbs.

About: Bounsweet smells good enough to eat—which sometimes gets it into trouble! The intensely sugary liquid it gives off can be diluted to bring the sweetness level down so people can drink it.

BRIONNE

Type: *Water*

Height & weight:
2'00"   38.6 lbs.

About: Brionne pelts its opponents with water balloons in a swift and skilful battle dance. It also shows off its dancing abilities when trying to cheer up its Trainer.

BRUXISH

Type: *Water-Psychic*

Height & weight:
2'11"   41.9 lbs.

About: Don't let the beguiling grin of the brightly colored Bruxish fool you—those teeth are strong and sharp, and it can wield psychic powers mighty enough to stun an opponent in battle.

BUZZWOLE

Type: *Bug-Fighting*

Height & weight:
7'10"   735.5 lbs.

About: Buzzwole, one of the mysterious Ultra Beasts, is enormously strong, capable of demolishing heavy machinery with a punch. When it displays its impressive muscles, no one is sure whether it's just showing off—or issuing a threat.

CELESTEELA

Type: Steel-Flying

Height & weight:
30'02" 2204.4 lbs.

About: Celesteela, one of the mysterious Ultra Beasts, can shoot incendiary gases from its arms and has been known to burn down wide swaths of trees. In flight, it can reach impressive speeds.

CHARJABUG

Type: Bug-Electric

Height & weight:
1'08" 23.1 lbs.

About: When Charjabug breaks down food for energy, some of that energy is stored as electricity inside its body. A Trainer who likes to go camping would appreciate having this Pokémon as a partner!

COMFEY

Type: Fairy

Height & weight:
0'04" 0.7 lbs.

About: Comfey collects flowers and attaches them to its vine, where they flourish and release a calming fragrance. Adding these flowers to bathwater makes for a relaxing soak.

COSMOEM

LEGENDARY

Type: Psychic

Height & weight:
0'04" 2204.4 lbs.

About: Cosmoem never moves, radiating a gentle warmth as it develops inside the hard shell that surrounds it. Long ago, people referred to it as the cocoon of the stars, and some still think its origins lie in another world.

COSMOG

LEGENDARY

Type: Psychic

Height & weight:
0'08" 0.2 lbs.

About: Cosmog reportedly came to the Alola region from another world, but its origins are shrouded in mystery. Known as the child of the stars, it grows by gathering dust from the atmosphere.

CRABOMINABLE

Type: Fighting-Ice

Height & weight:
5'07" 396.8 lbs.

About: Covered in warm fur, Crabominable evolved from Crabrawler that took their goal of aiming for the top a bit too literally and found themselves at the summit of icy mountains. They can detach their pincers and shoot them at foes.

CRABRAWLER

Type: Fighting

Height & weight:
2'00" 15.4 lbs.

About: Crabrawler is always looking for a fight, and it really hates to lose. Sometimes its pincers come right off because it uses them for punching so much! Fortunately, it can regrow them quickly.

CUTIEFLY

Type: Bug-Fairy

Height & weight:
0'04" 0.4 lbs.

About: Cutiefly can sense the aura of flowers and gauge when they're ready to bloom, so it always knows where to find fresh nectar. If you notice a swarm of these Pokémon following you around, you might have a floral aura!

DARTRIX

Type: Grass-Flying

Height & weight:
2'04" 35.3 lbs.

About: Dartrix is very conscious of its appearance and spends a lot of time keeping its wings clean. It can throw sharp-edged feathers, known as blade quills, with great accuracy.

DECIDUEYE

Type: Grass-Ghost

Height & weight:
5'03" 80.7 lbs.

About: A natural marksman, Decidueye can shoot its arrow quills with astonishing precision, hitting a tiny target a hundred yards away. It tends to be calm and collected, but sometimes panics if it's caught off guard.

DEWPIDER

Type: Water-Bug

Height & weight:
1'00" 8.8 lbs.

About: Mostly aquatic, Dewpider brings a water-bubble "helmet" along when it ventures onto the land to look for food. The bubble also lends extra power when it headbutts an opponent.

DHELMISE

Type: Ghost-Grass

Height & weight:
12'10" 463.0 lbs.

About: When Dhelmise swings its mighty anchor, even the biggest Pokémon have to watch out! It snags seaweed floating past on the waves and scavenges detritus from the seafloor to add to its body.

ALOLAN DIGLETT

Type: *Ground-Steel*

Height & weight:
0'08" 2.2 lbs.

About: The metal hairs that sprout from the top of Diglett's head can be used to communicate or to sense its surroundings. It can extend just those hairs aboveground to make sure everything is safe before emerging.

DRAMPA

Type: *Normal-Dragon*

Height & weight:
9'10" 407.9 lbs.

About: Even wild Drampa have a real soft spot for kids. Though they make their home far away in the mountains, they often come into town to visit and play with the local children.

ALOLAN DUGTRIO

Type: *Ground-Steel*

Height & weight:
2'04" 146.8 lbs.

About: Although Dugtrio's golden hair is shiny and beautiful, people aren't inclined to collect it when it falls—there are stories that doing so will bring bad luck. In Alola, this Pokémon is thought to represent the spirit of the land.

ALOLAN EXEGGUTOR

Type: *Grass-Dragon*

Height & weight:
35'09" 916.2 lbs.

About: In the tropical sun and sand, Exeggutor grows exceptionally tall, unlocking draconic powers hidden deep within. Trainers in Alola are proud of the tree-like Exeggutor and consider this to be its ideal form.

FOMANTIS

Type: *Grass*

Height & weight:
1'00" 3.3 lbs.

About: Fomantis sleeps the day away, basking in the sunlight. The sweet scent it gives off sometimes attracts Cutiefly to its hiding place. During the night, it seeks out a safe place to sleep for the next day.

ALOLAN GEODUDE

Type: *Rock-Electric*

Height & weight:
1'04" 44.8 lbs.

About: In the Alola region, Geodude are naturally magnetic, and their bodies are often covered in iron particles they've picked up while sleeping in the sand. Stepping on one can cause a nasty shock, so beachgoers keep a sharp eye out.

ALOLAN GOLEM

Type: Rock-Electric

Height & weight:
5'07"   696.7 lbs.

About: The rocks Golem fires from its back carry a strong electrical charge, so even a glancing blow can deliver a powerful shock. Sometimes it grabs a Geodude to fire instead.

GOLISOPOD

Type: Bug-Water

Height & weight:
6'07"   238.1 lbs.

About: When Golisopod has to battle, its six sharp-clawed arms are certainly up to the task. Most of the time, though, it lives quietly in underwater caves, where it meditates and avoids conflict.

ALOLAN GRAVELER

Type: Rock-Electric

Height & weight:
3'03"   231.5 lbs.

About: The crystals that appear on Graveler's body are the result of consuming dravite, a particularly tasty mineral. Graveler often fight over dravite deposits, crashing together with a sound like thunder.

ALOLAN GRIMER

Type: Poison-Dark

Height & weight:
2'04"   92.6 lbs.

About: Grimer's appearance in the Alola region developed after it was called upon to deal with a persistent garbage problem. Each crystal on its body is formed from dangerous toxins, and those toxins escape if a crystal falls off.

GRUBBIN

Type: Bug

Height & weight:
1'04"   9.7 lbs.

About: Grubbin have discovered that sticking close to Electric-type Pokémon offers some protection from the Flying types that often like to attack them! With their strong jaws, they can scrape away tree bark to get at the delicious sap underneath.

GUMSHOOS

Type: Normal

Height & weight:
2'04"   31.3 lbs.

About: Gumshoos displays amazing patience when it's on a stakeout, waiting to ambush its prey. It's a natural enemy of Rattata, but the two rarely interact because they're awake at different times.

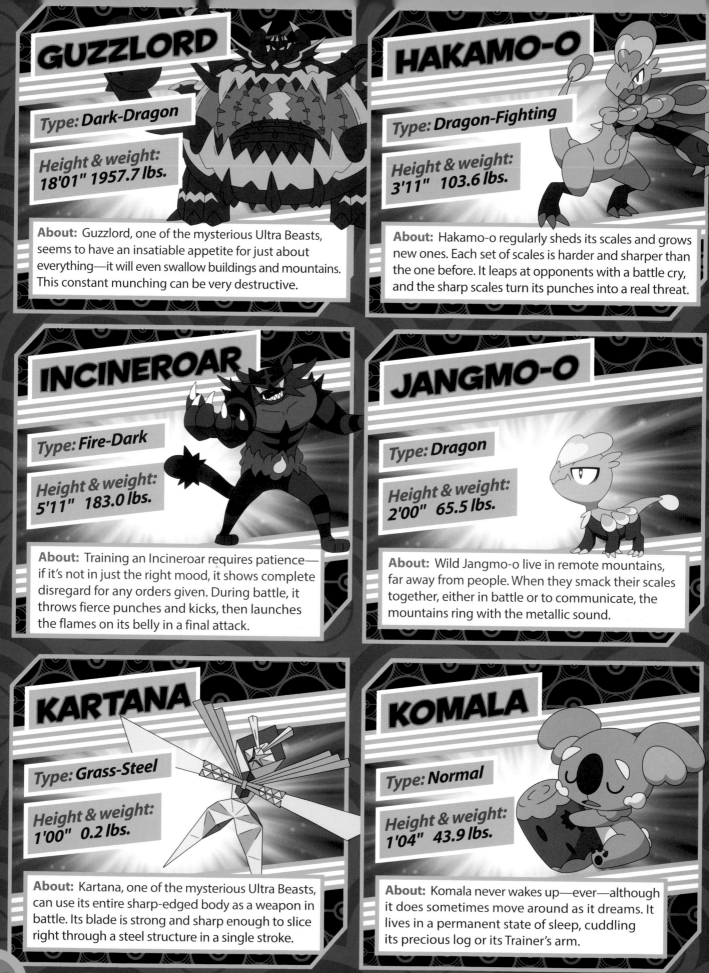

GUZZLORD

Type: *Dark-Dragon*

Height & weight:
18'01" 1957.7 lbs.

About: Guzzlord, one of the mysterious Ultra Beasts, seems to have an insatiable appetite for just about everything—it will even swallow buildings and mountains. This constant munching can be very destructive.

HAKAMO-O

Type: *Dragon-Fighting*

Height & weight:
3'11" 103.6 lbs.

About: Hakamo-o regularly sheds its scales and grows new ones. Each set of scales is harder and sharper than the one before. It leaps at opponents with a battle cry, and the sharp scales turn its punches into a real threat.

INCINEROAR

Type: *Fire-Dark*

Height & weight:
5'11" 183.0 lbs.

About: Training an Incineroar requires patience—if it's not in just the right mood, it shows complete disregard for any orders given. During battle, it throws fierce punches and kicks, then launches the flames on its belly in a final attack.

JANGMO-O

Type: *Dragon*

Height & weight:
2'00" 65.5 lbs.

About: Wild Jangmo-o live in remote mountains, far away from people. When they smack their scales together, either in battle or to communicate, the mountains ring with the metallic sound.

KARTANA

Type: *Grass-Steel*

Height & weight:
1'00" 0.2 lbs.

About: Kartana, one of the mysterious Ultra Beasts, can use its entire sharp-edged body as a weapon in battle. Its blade is strong and sharp enough to slice right through a steel structure in a single stroke.

KOMALA

Type: *Normal*

Height & weight:
1'04" 43.9 lbs.

About: Komala never wakes up—ever—although it does sometimes move around as it dreams. It lives in a permanent state of sleep, cuddling its precious log or its Trainer's arm.

KOMMO-O

Type: Dragon-Fighting

Height & weight:
5'03"   172.4 lbs.

About: Long ago, Kommo-o scales were collected and turned into weapons. For this Pokémon, the scales provide offense, defense, and even a warning system—when it shakes its tail, the scales clash together in a jangle that scares off weak opponents.

LITTEN

Type: Fire

Height & weight:
1'04"   9.5 lbs.

About: When it grooms its fur, Litten is storing up ammunition—the flaming fur is later coughed up in a fiery attack. Trainers often have a hard time getting this solitary Pokémon to trust them.

LUNALA

LEGENDARY

Type: Psychic-Ghost

Height & weight:
13'01"   264.6 lbs.

About: Lunala's wide wings soak up the light, plunging the brightest day into shadow. This Legendary Pokémon apparently makes its home in another world, and it returns there when its third eye becomes active.

LURANTIS

Type: Grass

Height & weight:
2'11"   40.8 lbs.

About: It can be difficult to give Lurantis the proper care to keep its coloring bright and vivid, but some Trainers enthusiastically accept the challenge. The beams it shoots from its petals can pierce thick metal.

LYCANROC (MIDDAY FORM)

Type: Rock

Height & weight:
2'07"   55.1 lbs.

About: Its thick mane conceals sharp rocks that it uses in battle along with its fangs and claws. Despite its fearsome arsenal, Lycanroc displays fierce loyalty toward a Trainer who has raised it well.

LYCANROC (MIDNIGHT FORM)

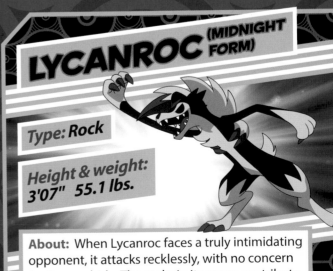

Type: Rock

Height & weight:
3'07"   55.1 lbs.

About: When Lycanroc faces a truly intimidating opponent, it attacks recklessly, with no concern for its own hide. The rocks in its mane contribute to the crushing power of its headbutt.

MAGEARNA

Type: Steel-Fairy

Height & weight:
3'03"   177.5 lbs.

About: Magearna was built many centuries ago by human inventors. The rest of this Pokémon's mechanical body is just a vehicle for its true self: the Soul-Heart contained in its chest.

MAREANIE

Type: Poison-Water

Height & weight:
1'04"   17.6 lbs.

About: Mareanie lives at the bottom of the sea or along the beach. It attacks with its head spike, which delivers poison that can weaken a foe. It's often tempted by the brightly colored coral of Corsola.

ALOLAN MAROWAK

Type: Fire-Ghost

Height & weight:
3'03"   75 lbs.

About: The flaming bone that Marowak spins like a baton once belonged to its mother, and it's protected by its mother's spirit. It grieves for its fallen companions, visiting their graves along the roadside.

ALOLAN MEOWTH

Type: Dark

Height & weight:
1'04"   9.3 lbs.

About: Meowth is very vain about the golden Charm on its forehead, becoming enraged if any dirt dulls its bright surface. These crafty Pokémon are not native to Alola, but thanks to human interference, their population has surged.

MIMIKYU

Type: Ghost-Fairy

Height & weight:
0'08"   1.5 lbs.

About: What does Mimikyu look like? No one really knows, but apparently it's terrifying—it always hides underneath an old rag so it doesn't scare anyone while it's trying to make friends.

MINIOR (METEOR FORM)

Type: Rock-Flying

Height & weight:
1'00"   88.2 lbs.

About: Minior came into being when tiny particles in the ozone layer underwent mutation. When its shell becomes too heavy, it falls to the ground, and the impact can knock its shell clean off.

MINIOR (RED CORE)

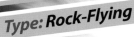

Type: Rock-Flying

Height & weight:
1'00"   0.7 lbs.

About: The atmospheric dust that Minior consumes influences the color of its core. When the core is exposed, it's extremely vulnerable, and Trainers are advised to get it into a Poké Ball for protection.

MORELULL

Type: Grass-Fairy

Height & weight:
0'08"   3.3 lbs.

About: The spores that Morelull gives off flicker with a hypnotic light that sends viewers to sleep. During the day, it plants itself beside a tree to absorb nutrients from the roots while it naps.

MUDBRAY

Type: Ground

Height & weight:
3'03"   242.5 lbs.

About: Mudbray just loves to get dirty, but it isn't just for fun. Playing in the mud actually gives it better traction for running—when its hooves are covered in dirt, they're less likely to slip, and it can run faster.

MUDSDALE

Type: Ground

Height & weight:
8'02"   2028.3 lbs.

About: With the help of the mud that coats its hooves, Mudsdale can deliver heavy kicks powerful enough to demolish a big truck. The mud it produces is weather-resistant, and people used to use it to shore up their houses.

ALOLAN MUK

Type: Poison-Dark

Height & weight:
3'03"   114.6 lbs.

About: Muk's bright and colorful markings are the result of chemical changes in its body, caused by its diet of all sorts of garbage. It's generally a pleasant and friendly companion, but if it gets hungry, it can turn destructive.

NECROZMA

LEGENDARY

Type: Psychic

Height & weight:
7'10"   507.1 lbs.

About: Some think Necrozma arrived from another world many eons ago. When it emerges from its underground slumber, it seems to absorb light for use as energy to power its laser-like blasts.

NIHILEGO

Type: *Rock-Poison*

Height & weight:
3'11" 122.4 lbs.

About: Nihilego, one of the mysterious Ultra Beasts, can apparently infest other beings and incite them to violence. Research is inconclusive as to whether this Pokémon can think for itself, but it sometimes exhibits the behavior of a young girl.

ALOLAN NINETALES

Type: *Ice-Fairy*

Height & weight:
3'07" 43.9 lbs.

About: In its frosty coat, Ninetales creates ice droplets that can be used to shower over opponents. It's generally calm and collected, but if it becomes angry, it can freeze the offenders in their tracks.

ORANGURU

Type: *Normal-Psychic*

Height & weight:
4'11" 167.6 lbs.

About: Extremely intelligent and somewhat particular, Oranguru can be a bad fit for Trainers who lack experience. In the wild, it spends most of its time in the jungle canopy, though it sometimes emerges in search of an intellectual challenge.

ORICORIO (BAILE STYLE)

Type: *Fire-Flying*

Height & weight:
2'00" 7.5 lbs.

About: Drinking red nectar gives Oricorio a fiery style when it dances. It's best to enjoy this beautiful performance from a distance, because its beating wings give off scorching flames.

ORICORIO (PA'U STYLE)

Type: *Psychic-Flying*

Height & weight:
2'00" 7.5 lbs.

About: Drinking pink nectar transforms Oricorio into a hypnotically swaying dancer. As its opponents watch, entranced, the swaying movement relaxes Oricorio's mind so it can build up psychic energy for attacks.

ORICORIO (POM-POM STYLE)

Type: *Electric-Flying*

Height & weight:
2'00" 7.5 lbs.

About: Drinking yellow nectar makes Oricorio's dance style truly electric. The charge generated by the rubbing of its feathers allows it to land shocking punches in battle as it performs a cheerful dance.

ORICORIO (SENSU STYLE)

Type: Ghost-Flying

Height & weight:
2'00"   7.5 lbs.

About: Drinking purple nectar inspires Oricorio to perform a dreamy and elegant dance. The spirits of the departed are drawn to this beautiful performance, and Oricorio channels their power into its attacks.

PALOSSAND

Type: Ghost-Ground

Height & weight:
4'03"   551.2 lbs.

About: In order to evolve, this Pokémon took control of people playing in the sand to build up its body into a sand castle. Those who disappear can sometimes be found buried underneath Palossand, drained of their vitality.

PASSIMIAN

Type: Fighting

Height & weight:
6'07"   182.5 lbs.

About: Passimian are real team players—they learn from one another and work together for the benefit of the group. Each group, composed of about twenty Passimian, shares a remarkably strong bond.

ALOLAN PERSIAN

Type: Dark

Height & weight:
3'07"   72.8 lbs.

About: Trainers in Alola adore Persian for its coat, which is very smooth and has a velvety texture. This Pokémon has developed a haughty attitude and prefers to fight dirty when it gets into battle.

PHEROMOSA

Type: Bug-Fighting

Height & weight:
5'11"   55.1 lbs.

About: Pheromosa, one of the mysterious Ultra Beasts, seems to be extremely wary of germs and won't touch anything willingly. Witnesses have seen it charging through the region at amazing speeds.

PIKIPEK

Type: Normal-Flying

Height & weight:
1'00"   2.6 lbs.

About: Pikipek can drill into the side of a tree at the rate of sixteen pecks per second! It uses the resulting hole as a place to nest and to store berries—both for food and for ammunition.

POPPLIO

Type: *Water*

Height & weight:
1'04" 16.5 lbs.

About: Popplio uses the water balloons it blows from its nose as weapons in battle. It's a hard worker and puts in lots of practice creating and controlling these balloons.

PRIMARINA

Type: *Water-Fairy*

Height & weight:
5'11" 97.0 lbs.

About: This Pokémon's singing voice is a delicate and powerful weapon, used to attack its foes and to control the water balloons it creates. Groups of Primarina teach these battle songs to the next generation.

PYUKUMUKU

Type: *Water*

Height & weight:
1'00" 2.6 lbs.

About: Pyukumuku has a remarkable and revolting weapon in battle: it can spew out its innards to strike at its opponent. It's covered in a sticky slime that beachgoers use to soothe their skin after a sunburn.

ALOLAN RAICHU

Type: *Electric-Psychic*

Height & weight:
2'04" 46.3 lbs.

About: Researchers speculate that Raichu looks different in the Alola region because of what it eats. It can "surf" on its own tail, standing on the flat surface and using psychic power to raise itself off the ground.

ALOLAN RATICATE

Type: *Dark-Normal*

Height & weight:
2'04" 56.2 lbs.

About: Each Raticate leads a group of Rattata, and the groups regularly scuffle over food. This Pokémon is rather picky about what it eats, so a restaurant where a Raticate lives is likely to be a good one.

ALOLAN RATTATA

Type: *Dark-Normal*

Height & weight:
1'00" 8.4 lbs.

About: Rattata sleep during the day and spend their nights searching for the best food to bring back to the Raticate who leads them. They use their strong teeth to gnaw their way into people's kitchens.

RIBOMBEE

Type: Bug-Fairy

Height & weight: 0'08"   1.1 lbs.

About: Ribombee gathers up pollen and forms it into a variety of puffs with different effects. Some enhance battle skills and can be used as supplements, while others deliver excellent nutrition.

ROCKRUFF

Type: Rock

Height & weight: 1'08"   20.3 lbs.

About: Rockruff has a long history of living in harmony with people. This friendly Pokémon is often recommended for Trainers just starting their journey, although it tends to develop a bit of a wild side as it grows.

ROWLET

Type: Grass-Flying

Height & weight: 1'00"   3.3 lbs.

About: During the day, Rowlet rests and generates energy via photosynthesis. In the night, it flies silently to sneak up on foes and launch a flurry of kicking attacks.

SALANDIT

Type: Poison-Fire

Height & weight: 2'00"   10.6 lbs.

About: Salandit gives off a toxic gas that causes dizziness and confusion when inhaled. It uses this gas to distract opponents before attacking. These Pokémon can often be found living on the slopes of volcanoes.

SALAZZLE

Type: Poison-Fire

Height & weight: 3'11"   48.9 lbs.

About: Apparently, all Salazzle are female. They tend to attract several male Salandit and live together in a group. The poisonous gas they give off contains powerful pheromones and is sometimes used as a perfume ingredient.

ALOLAN SANDSHREW

Type: Ice-Steel

Height & weight: 2'04"   88.2 lbs.

About: Sandshrew lives high in the snowy mountains of Alola, where it has developed a shell of thick steel. It's very good at sliding across the ice—whether it does so under its own power or as part of a Sandshrew-sliding contest!

ALOLAN SANDSLASH

Type: *Ice-Steel*

Height & weight:
3'11"   121.3 lbs.

About: Sandslash is covered in spikes of tough steel, and in the cold mountains where it lives, each spike develops a thick coating of ice. A plume of snow flies up behind it as it dashes across the snowfield.

SANDYGAST

Type: *Ghost-Ground*

Height & weight:
1'08"   154.3 lbs.

About: A child created a mound of sand while playing on the beach, and it became a Sandygast. Putting your hand in its mouth is a sure way to fall prey to its mind control.

SHIINOTIC

Type: *Grass-Fairy*

Height & weight:
3'03"   25.4 lbs.

About: It's a bad idea to wander in Shiinotic's forest home at night. The strange, flickering lights given off by this Pokémon's spores can confuse travelers and cause them to lose their way.

SOLGALEO
LEGENDARY

Type: *Psychic-Steel*

Height & weight:
11'02"   507.1 lbs.

About: Solgaleo's entire body radiates a bright light that can wipe away the darkness of night. This Legendary Pokémon apparently makes its home in another world, and it returns there when its third eye becomes active.

STEENEE

Type: *Grass*

Height & weight:
2'04"   18.1 lbs.

About: Lively and cheerful, Steenee often attracts a crowd of other Pokémon drawn to its energy and its lovely scent. Its sepals have evolved into a hard shell to protect its head and body from attackers.

STUFFUL

Type: *Normal-Fighting*

Height & weight:
1'08"   15.0 lbs.

About: Petting an unfamiliar Stufful is a bad idea, even though it's really cute—it dislikes being touched by anyone it doesn't consider a friend, and responds with a flailing of limbs that can knock over a strong fighter.

TAPU BULU

LEGENDARY

Type: Grass-Fairy

Height & weight:
6'03"   100.3 lbs.

About: Tapu Bulu has a reputation for laziness—rather than battling directly, it commands vines to pin down its foes. The plants that grow abundantly in its wake give it energy. It's known as the guardian of Ula'ula Island.

TAPU FINI

LEGENDARY

Type: Water-Fairy

Height & weight:
4'03"   46.7 lbs.

About: Tapu Fini can control and cleanse water, washing away impurities. When threatened, it summons a dense fog to confuse its enemies. This Pokémon draws energy from ocean currents. It's known as the guardian of Poni Island.

TAPU KOKO

LEGENDARY

Type: Electric-Fairy

Height & weight:
5'11"   45.2 lbs.

About: Somewhat lacking in attention span, Tapu Koko is quick to anger but just as quickly forgets why it's angry. Calling thunderclouds lets it store up lightning as energy. It's known as the guardian of Melemele Island.

TAPU LELE

LEGENDARY

Type: Psychic-Fairy

Height & weight:
3'11"   41.0 lbs.

About: As Tapu Lele flutters through the air, people in search of good health gather up the glowing scales that fall from its body. It draws energy from the scent of flowers. It's known as the guardian of Akala Island.

TOGEDEMARU

Type: Electric-Steel

Height & weight:
1'00"   7.3 lbs.

About: Its back is covered with long, spiny fur that usually lies flat. Togedemaru can bristle up the fur during battle for use as a weapon, or during storms to attract lightning, which it stores as electricity in its body.

TORRACAT

Type: Fire

Height & weight:
2'04"   55.1 lbs.

About: Torracat attacks with powerful punches from its front legs, which are strong enough to bend iron. When it spits flames, the fiery bell at its throat starts to ring.

TOUCANNON

Type: *Normal-Flying*

Height & weight:
3'07"   57.3 lbs.

About: The inside of Toucannon's beak gets very hot during a battle—over two hundred degrees Fahrenheit. The heat fuels its explosive seed-shooting and can also cause serious burns to its opponent.

TOXAPEX

Type: *Poison-Water*

Height & weight:
2'04"   32.0 lbs.

About: It's a good thing Toxapex lives at the bottom of the ocean, because its poison is very dangerous. Those who fall prey to it can expect three very painful days before they recover, and the effects can linger.

TRUMBEAK

Type: *Normal-Flying*

Height & weight:
2'00"   32.6 lbs.

About: Trumbeak stores berry seeds in its beak to use as ammunition. It attacks opponents with a rapid-fire burst of seeds. Its beak is also very good at making lots of noise!

TSAREENA

Type: *Grass*

Height & weight:
3'11"   47.2 lbs.

About: Beauty salons sometimes use images of the lovely Tsareena in their advertising. It can be a fierce fighter, using its long legs to deliver skillful kicks as it mocks its defeated opponent.

TURTONATOR

Type: *Fire-Dragon*

Height & weight:
6'07"   467.4 lbs.

About: Poisonous gases and flames spew from Turtonator's nostrils. Its shell is made of unstable material that might explode upon impact, so opponents are advised to aim for its stomach instead.

VIKAVOLT

Type: *Bug-Electric*

Height & weight:
4'11"   99.2 lbs.

About: Vikavolt uses its large jaws to focus the electricity it produces inside its body, then unleashes a powerful zap to stun its opponents. Flying-type Pokémon that once posed a threat are no match for its shocking attacks.

ALOLAN VULPIX

Type: *Ice*

Height & weight:
2'00"   21.8 lbs.

About: Vulpix in the Alola region were once known as Keokeo, and some older folks still use that name. Its six tails can create a spray of ice crystals to cool itself off when it gets too hot.

WIMPOD

Type: *Bug-Water*

Height & weight:
1'08"   26.5 lbs.

About: When the cowardly Wimpod flees from battle, it leaves a path swept clean by the passing of its many legs. It helps keep the beaches and seabeds clean, too, scavenging just about anything edible.

WISHIWASHI (SOLO FORM)

Type: *Water*

Height & weight:
0'08"   0.7 lbs.

About: If a Wishiwashi looks like it's about to cry, watch out! The light that shines from its watering eyes draws the entire school, and they band together to fight off their opponent by sheer strength of numbers.

WISHIWASHI (SCHOOL FORM)

Type: *Water*

Height & weight:
0'08"   26'11"

About: On its own, Wishiwashi is a feeble opponent, but when many Wishiwashi come together in a school, they are known as the demon of the sea. Their combined power is enough to scare away a Gyarados.

XURKITREE

Type: *Electric*

Height & weight:
12'06"   220.5 lbs.

About: Xurkitree, one of the mysterious Ultra Beasts, invaded an electric plant after it emerged from the Ultra Wormhole. Some suspect it absorbs electricity into its body to power the serious shocks it gives off.

YUNGOOS

Type: *Normal*

Height & weight:
1'04"   13.2 lbs.

About: Yungoos is always on the move during the day, looking for food—and it's not too picky about what it bites with its sharp teeth. When night comes, it immediately falls asleep no matter where it happens to be.

A GOOD TRAINER KNOWS WHICH POKÉMON TO CATCH AND USE IN BATTLE AND WHICH TO AVOID ALTOGETHER! READY TO TEST YOUR SKILLS? TRY THE QUIZ ON PAGES 44–45.

AMAZING EVOLUTIONS

Nothing stays the same for long in the Alola region—certainly not the Pokémon that live there! Professor Kukui has mixed up these evolution chains. Write the numbers in the boxes to the order in which the Pokémon evolve.

1
A Litten
B Incineroar
C Torracat

A   C   B

2
A Decidueye
B Dartrix
Rowlet C

C   B   A

3
A Brionne
B Primarina
C Popplio

C   A   B

4
Toucannon A
B Trumbeak
C Pikipek

C   B   A

42

5
- **A** Vikavolt
- **C** Charjabug
- **B** Grubbin

C B A

6
- **A** Steenee
- **B** Bounsweet
- **C** Tsareena

AB A C

7
- **A** Golem
- **B** Graveler
- **C** Geodude

C B A

8
- **A** Jangmo-o
- **B** Kommo-o
- **C** Hakamo-o

A C B

The answers are on page 78.

POKÉMON SCHOOL QUIZ

Students at the Pokémon School work hard to learn all they can about Pokémon. Trainers' knowledge is the key to success in battles!

Try these questions set by Principal Oak and Professor Kukui. Answer at least seven out of ten questions correctly and you'll earn yourself a place at the Pokémon School!

1

THIS POKÉMON IS KNOWN AS THE SCRATCH CAT.

A. True ☑

B. False ☐

2

WHAT POKÉMON DOES STUFFUL EVOLVE INTO?

A. Clefable ☐

B. Bewear ☑

C. Solgaleo ☐

3

WHAT TYPE OF POKÉMON IS LITTEN?

A. Normal ☐

B. Fire ☑

C. Ghost ☐

4

IS THIS LYRANROC'S MIDDAY OR MIDNIGHT FORM?

A. Midday ☐

B. Midnight ☑

WHICH OF THE FOLLOWING IS A BUG-TYPE POKÉMON?

A. Bounsweet ☐

B. Bruxish ☐

C. Grubbin ☑

WHAT CAUSES ALOLAN MUK TO LOOK SO COLORFUL?

A. *The tropical sunlight* ☐

B. *Drinking the Alolan seawater* ☐

C. *Its diet of garbage* ☐

WHICH POKÉMON NEVER WAKES UP?

A. *Komala* ☑

B. *Rattata* ☐

C. *Yungoos* ☐

WHICH TYPE OF POKÉMON IS LUNALA?

A. *Mythical* ☐

B. *Legendary* ☑

WHICH POKÉMON IS THE GUARDIAN OF MELEMELE ISLAND?

A. *Tapu Fini* ☐

B. *Tapu Lele* ☐

C. *Tapu Koko* ☑

D. *Tapu Bulu* ☐

WHICH POKÉMON CAN REGROW ITS LIMBS?

A. *Crabrawler* ☐

B. *Marowak* ☐

C. *Salandit* ☐

The answers are on page 78.

WHO'S THAT POKÉMON?

The Alola region is home to plenty of Pokémon that Ash and Pikachu have never met before.

Draw lines to match the Pokémon to their shadows.

Now circle the little Alolan Sandshrew

G

H

I

J

K

L

GRUBBIN!

When Ash first met Grubbin, the Bug-type Pokémon went wild and nipped Ash on the nose!

Follow these steps to draw Grubbin.

1

Start by drawing swirls to show the detail on Grubbin's head, then draw an extra line that will form the Pokémon's back leg.

2 Now draw the jaws and feelers, with lines for the tips.

3

Next, draw the detail for one of Grubbin's eyes.

4

Draw Grubbin's front legs, the details on its body, then add a couple spots. Rub out any mistakes.

5

Great work! Now color in your Pokémon using the colors shown below.

THE GUARDIAN'S CHALLENGE

A sh and Pikachu were loving life in the Alola region. It was time for Ash to take a huge step on his quest to become a Pokémon Master!

It was the start of another day at the Pokémon School, but today, the class had a new pupil . . . Professor Kukui entered the room, followed by Ash and Pikachu.

"Alola!" the professor greeted his class.

"Starting today, Ash will be joining us. Let's make him feel welcome."

"I really want to become a Pokémon Master," Ash smiled. "I'm going to learn everything about this place!"

Ash's new classmates smiled back, all except Kiawe. He had spotted the Z-Ring on Ash's wrist.

Mallow saw it, too. "Whoa, Ash," she gasped. "Is that a Z-Crystal?"

"That's so cool!" Sophocles added.

But Kiawe wasn't impressed. "Where did you get that? You didn't complete the Island Challenge Trials," he said, frowning.

"Tapu Koko gave it to me," Ash replied. He began to tell the class about how he had met the spirit guardian.

Kiawe was puzzled. "Tapu Koko? How could it have gotten a Z-Ring?"

"Tapu Koko is a mysterious Pokémon," said Lillie. "I read that sometimes it will give gifts to people it likes."

"It must love Ash then!" Mallow smiled.

Sophocles explained that Kiawe had gotten his Z-Ring by passing the grand trial on Akala Island. Ash was excited!

"Does this mean I can use Z-Moves, like you?" Ash asked Kiawe.

"Z-Moves should not be taken lightly," Kiawe warned. "Only when a Pokémon and its Trainer's hearts become one will the Z-Ring turn their feelings into power."

Ash was quiet.

"Those feelings must be about something greater than themselves," Kiawe went on. "Like helping the islanders . . . or helping Pokémon. Only those who care about all living things are permitted to use Z-Moves. I'm not exactly sure what Tapu Koko saw in you, but as a Z-Ring owner, you need to realize your responsibility."

Ash looked at the Z-Ring. "Kiawe," he began, "I know how special the Z-Moves are; you can count on me."

"That's good enough for me," Kiawe said, smiling.

The next day, Ash's new classmates decided to throw a surprise welcome party for Ash and Pikachu. It was set to be a day full of surprises.

First, Sophocles had a special party game for Ash and Pikachu.

"Whichever team pops all the balloons first wins!" Sophocles smiled. He was sure that he and his Pokémon, Togedemaru, would win easily.

Ash and Pikachu started slowly. Popping the balloons wasn't as easy as it looked . . . so Pikachu decided to use Thunderbolt. But to their surprise, Togedemaru absorbed the lightning bolts with its spines, and released them itself to pop the balloons.

"The winners are Togedemaru and Sophocles!" Mallow announced.

Lillie and Popplio were up against Ash and Pikachu in the next game. In a Pokémon Aquathlon, the Trainer must run while the Pokémon swims.

Pikachu swam strongly, and soon the finish line was in sight. There was no sign of Popplio . . . until it suddenly zoomed out of nowhere to beat Pikachu to the finish line. Lillie and her Pokémon were the winners!

"Popplio can swim at speeds of twenty-five miles per hour." Lillie smiled proudly.

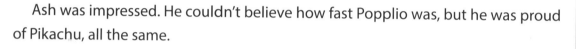

Ash was impressed. He couldn't believe how fast Popplio was, but he was proud of Pikachu, all the same.

In the next game, Ash was narrowly beaten by Kiawe in a Tauros race. Ash may have lost the race, but he'd had fun. Riding a three-tailed Tauros was awesome!

The friends had built up quite an appetite completing the morning's challenges. It was time to head to Mallow's family's restaurant to refuel.

"De-lish!" said Ash, gobbling up his lunch. Mallow sure knew how to cook up a Pokémon feast!

Suddenly, there was a loud, "*CAW, CAW!*" It was a sound that Ash had heard before. Tapu Koko!

Tapu Koko darted into the restaurant. It was so fast, Ash's eyes couldn't keep up. It flew off into the forest, taking's Ash's cap with it. Ash and Pikachu chased after the guardian. His friends followed, too.

"Ash, slow down!" called Mallow.

MEMORY GAME

Trainers need a sharp memory!

Study the picture for sixty seconds, then turn the page and try to answer as many questions as you can.

1 On which wrist was Ash's Z-Ring?

2 What color Berry was Pikachu eating?

3 What was Kiawe holding?

4 Which Normal- and Flying-type Pokémon did you see?

5 Which Pokémon was hiding in the long grass?

6 How many golden hairs were on Diglett's head?

7 Which island guardian was in the scene?

8 Which Pokémon was collecting pollen?

The answers are on page 78.
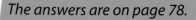

DINNERTIME DOUBLE

There are eight differences between these dinnertime scenes. Can you spot them all?

A

B

Color in a Berry for each difference you find.

The answers are on page 78.

SOMETHING STRANGE

What's wrong with this Alola scene?
Circle ten things that look strange in the picture below.

The answers are on page 78.

TRIVIA TIME!

Can you answer these five questions about Alolan Pokémon?

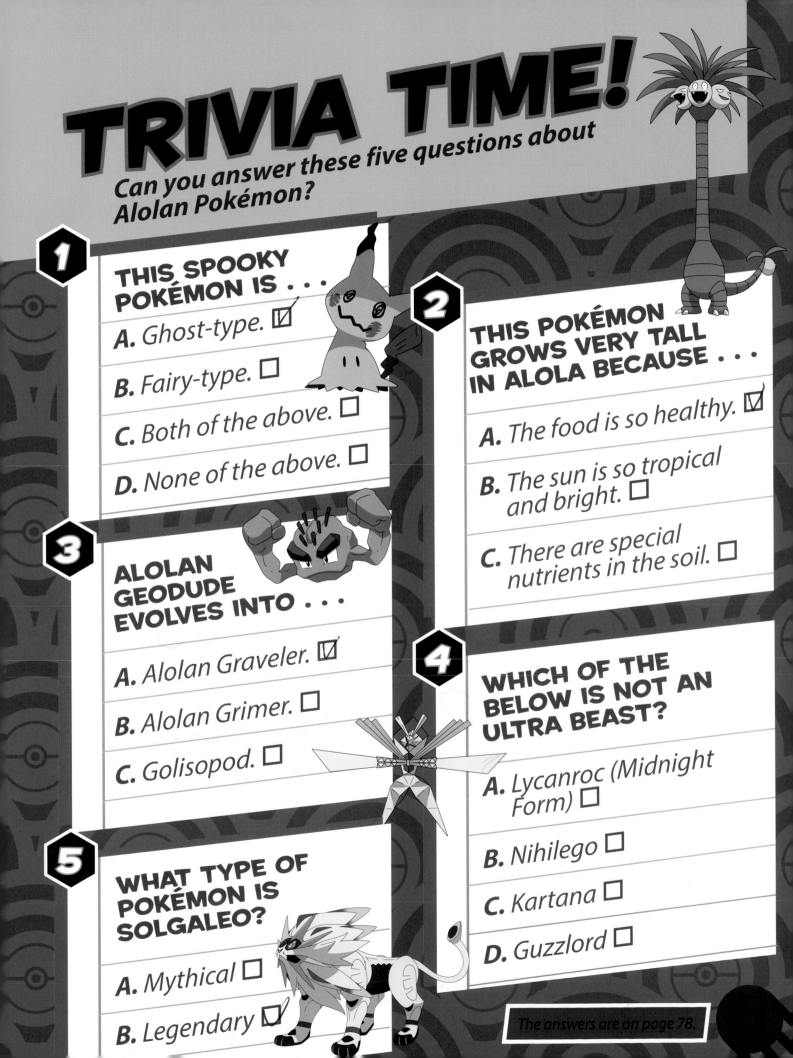

1 THIS SPOOKY POKÉMON IS . . .

A. Ghost-type. ☑

B. Fairy-type. ☐

C. Both of the above. ☐

D. None of the above. ☐

2 THIS POKÉMON GROWS VERY TALL IN ALOLA BECAUSE . . .

A. The food is so healthy. ☑

B. The sun is so tropical and bright. ☐

C. There are special nutrients in the soil. ☐

3 ALOLAN GEODUDE EVOLVES INTO . . .

A. Alolan Graveler. ☑

B. Alolan Grimer. ☐

C. Golisopod. ☐

4 WHICH OF THE BELOW IS NOT AN ULTRA BEAST?

A. Lycanroc (Midnight Form) ☐

B. Nihilego ☐

C. Kartana ☐

D. Guzzlord ☐

5 WHAT TYPE OF POKÉMON IS SOLGALEO?

A. Mythical ☐

B. Legendary ☑

The answers are on page 78.

POKÉMON PATTERNS

Check out these Pokémon patterns!
Write the name of the Pokémon that should come next in each row.
You can even try drawing them!

1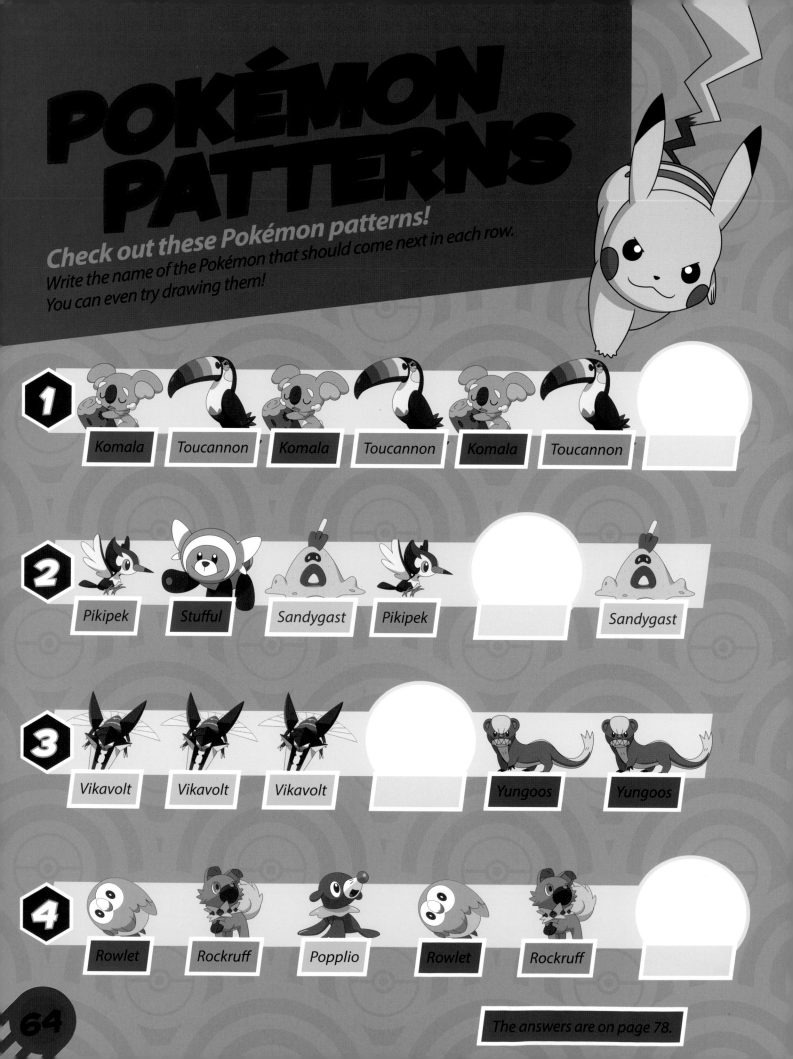

Komala | Toucannon | Komala | Toucannon | Komala | Toucannon |

2

Pikipek | Stuffful | Sandygast | Pikipek | | Sandygast

3

Vikavolt | Vikavolt | Vikavolt | | Yungoos | Yungoos

4

Rowlet | Rockruff | Popplio | Rowlet | Rockruff |

The answers are on page 78.

5 — Muk · Muk · ? · Muk · Muk · Litten

6 — Mimikyu · Pikachu · Pikachu · Mimikyu · ? · Pikachu · Mimikyu

7 — Alolan Vulpix · ? · Alolan Vulpix · Togedemaru · Alolan Vulpix · Togedemaru

8 — Litten · Torracat · Incineroar · Litten · ? · Incineroar

9 — Comfey · Comfey · ? · Comfey · Comfey · Bounsweet

10 — Alolan Diglett · Pyukumuku · Alolan Rattata · Alolan Diglett · ? · Alolan Rattata

CHAMPION'S CROSSWORD

How many of these puzzling Pokémon clues can you work out?
Complete the crossword to become a true Pokémon champion!

3. p i k a c h u

ACROSS

1. The Pokémon School is situated on this Alolan island. (8)

5. This Fire-type Pokémon spits red-hot furballs. (6)

7. The guardian of Akala Island. (4, 4)

8. The first name of Principal Oak, Samuel Oak's cousin. (6)

9. Use this Poké Ball to catch a Pokémon at night or in the dark. (4, 4)

10. Stuffal evolves into this Fighting-type Pokémon. (6)

DOWN

2. A large Pokémon known as the "beast that calls the moon." (6)

3. The name of Ash's best buddy. Easy! (7)

4. The color of Water-type Pokémon, Popplio. (4)

6. Kiawe's devasting Pokémon with a super-hard shell. (10)

TARGET PRACTICE

Ash is fired up for battle!

Close your eyes and draw twelve Xs on the page.
Then open your eyes and see how many Pokémon you caught.

Count your hits to see how you scored.

0–3

Time to enroll at Pokémon School!

4–7

Work on your strategy—those Pokémon are sneaky.

8–10

Pretty good work! Keep going.

11–12

Awesome, you're a top Trainer!

CREATURE COUNT

Ash has been busy catching every new Pokémon he can find in the Alola region!

Take a look at the pictures in the box and count how many of each Pokémon he has caught. Write the correct number in each box.

Charjabug

Mudbray

Litten

Turtonator

Komala

Drampa

Bewear

Cutiefly

Alolan Raichu

The answers are on page 79.

ANSWERS

PAGE 12
1. C 2. F 3. E 4. A 5. H 6. D 7. B 8. J 9. G
10. I

PAGE 13

PAGES 42–43
1. A, C, B 2. C, B, A
3. C, A, B 4. C, B, A
5. B, C, A 6. B, A, C
7. C, B, A 8. A, C, B

PAGES 44–45
1. A – True 2. B – Bewear 3. B – Fire
4. B – Midnight 5. C – Grubbin 6. C – Its diet of
garbage 7. A – Komala 8. B – Legendary
9. C – Tapu Koko 10. A – Crabrawler

PAGES 46–47

PAGE 58
1. Togedemaru 2. Charjabug 3. Raichu
4. Vikavolt

PAGE 60
1. left 2. blue 3. Poké Ball 4. Toucannon,
5. Charjabug 6. three 7. Tapu Lele 8. Ribombee

PAGE 61

PAGE 62

PAGE 63

1. C 2. B 3. A 4. A 5. B

PAGE 64

Komala   Stufful   Yungoos   Popplio

PAGE 65

Litten   Pikachu   Togedemaru   Torracat

Bounsweet   Pyukumuku

PAGE 66

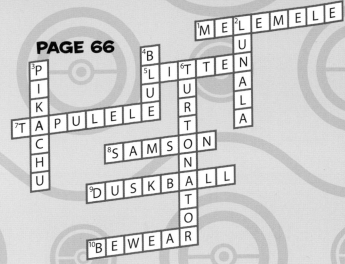

Crossword answers:
- 1. MELEMELE
- 2. LUNALA
- 3. PIKACHU
- 4. BLUE
- 5. LITTEN
- 6. TURTONATOR
- 7. TAPULELE
- 8. SAMSON
- 9. DUSKBALL
- 10. BEWEAR

PAGE 73

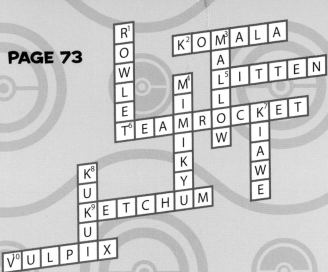

Crossword answers:
- 1. ROWLET
- 2. KOMALA
- 3. KALLOW
- 4. MIKY
- 5. LITTEN
- 6. TEAMROCKET
- 7. KIAWE
- 8. KUKU
- 9. KETCHUM
- V. VULPIX

PAGE 68

Komala – 5, Charjabug – 3, Mudbray – 4, Litten – 4, Turtonator – 1, Drampa – 3, Bewear – 4, Cutiefly – 8, Alolan Raichu – 5

PAGE 69

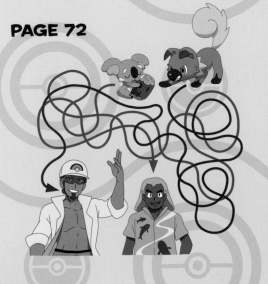

PAGE 70–71

1. C   2. B   3. B   4. C   5. B   6. C   7. A   8. D
9. B   10. A

PAGE 72

PAGE 74

PAGE 75

1. Mareanie   2. Dewpider   3. Bruxish   4. Brionne

PAGE 76–77

1. Pyukumuku
2. Alolan Dugtrio
3. Gumshoos
4. Mareanie
5. Palossand
6. Sandygast

FAREWELL

Thanks for completing these challenges, Trainer! You're well on your way to completing your Pokémon quest.